DETECTIVE GORDON

illustrated by Gitte Spee

THE FIRST CASE

by

Ulf Nilsson

GECKO PRESS

CHAPTER ONE

Stolen nuts.
Suspects: everyone.

"Wretched thieves!" cried a small creature as it scurried through the snow. "Thieving wretches!"

It was late in the evening and the whole forest was asleep.

It was snowing softly and beautifully.

"Monstrous plunderers!" called the little animal in a trembling, squeaky voice. "Plundering monsters!"

The animal came to a path. The path led to a little house. And the little house was a police station. A light shone in the window, as it always did at the police station.

The animal brushed the snow from its coat and shook a swirl of flakes from its long furry tail. It was a squirrel, which now wiped its feet and stepped inside.

"Hoo! Horrible and sad!" cried the squirrel. "Sadness and horror!"

The squirrel looked around. It was a completely ordinary police station. First you entered the big police room. On the wall beside the door was a glass cabinet. In the cabinet was a pistol and a baton. The glass was very thick and the cabinet was locked with a strong lock.

In the middle of the big police room was a fireplace where a few embers glowed. Behind the fireplace was a little kitchen for making tea.

The police station had many modern gadgets the squirrel didn't understand. It was a strange house, full of odd things, he thought. The squirrel himself lived in a hole in a tree. He had no chairs, tables, and suchlike. It was just him and his nuts, which was all he needed.

Then the squirrel noticed three very large cake tins. He smelled something agreeable and he looked at them with interest.

The squirrel turned to the right. There was the prison with its barred door, standing open. Inside, a bed was made up with a thick quilt and two pillows. Clearly no thieves were staying at the moment.

He turned to the left. There was another small room: a bedroom for the chief of police. The squirrel peered in through a gap in the doorway. Above the bed were pictures of toads—old toads, very small toads, and some the squirrel found quite ugly. Then he went right in and stood before a big desk. A very fat toad sat at the desk with an important piece of paper in front of him and a pen in his hand.

This was the famous Detective Gordon, chief of police and chief of detectives in the forest. The famous Chief Detective Gordon, feared by all criminals.

But Detective Gordon was asleep. He lay on his important paper, his face in a small pile of cake crumbs. His mouth was open and he was snoring. From the corner of his mouth, spit dribbled onto the paper.

"Hoo!" said the squirrel once more.

The detective twitched, mumbled a little, and licked his lips in his sleep. Then he rubbed his big round eyes. He suddenly seemed to be wide awake.

"I wasn't asleep!" he said quickly. "I was writing something important."

He looked at the paper. It was wet and everything he had written was smudged. Smudged, with cake crumbs on it. "But it didn't turn out so well," he added sadly, crumpling up the paper. "My dear squirrel, please sit here on the visitors' stool. How can I help?"

The squirrel sat carefully on the little stool and started to explain. It was a long and convoluted story which took a long time to begin and seemed to have no end. More and more people turned up in the story, did nothing, and then disappeared. A great many were suspected of a crime.

But what crime was it?

No ordinary person would be able to understand what it was all about.

And yet, Detective Gordon did.

By the end, the squirrel was so upset he began to cry. Detective Gordon gave him a handkerchief, but didn't interrupt. He never did. Sometimes he said a small "Uh-huh" to help the squirrel along. After three-quarters of an hour Detective Gordon wrote on a new, dry piece of paper:

Nuts stolen
from squirrel.
Suspects: no one.
Or suspects:
everyone!

The squirrel finally finished his story and he sat sniffling quietly, stroking his nose with his tail to comfort himself. He had a soft nose and mild, sensitive eyes. The detective was a little envious.

The detective had two drawers in his desk. One was for important notes, the other for his stamp. The detective took out the big old-fashioned stamp, placed it on the paper, moved it a little to the right and then a little to the left. Then he pressed. Kla-dunk, it went.

At that, the squirrel grew calm and seemed satisfied.

That was a very good stamp, Detective Gordon thought.

The squirrel twisted the handkerchief in his hands.

"Will I get my nuts back?" he asked.

"I'll investigate the case."

They went out together into the snow. It was snowing still, and the full moon was perched in the treetops, spreading its light. The squirrel said he could show the way. Detective Gordon shook his head.

He knew how to follow tracks. After all, he was a detective!

CHAPTER TWO

Guarding the hole.
Nothing happens. Yes, it does!

Detective Gordon actually could read tracks in snow. He could see that a squirrel had made its way to the police station quite recently, maybe three-quarters of an hour ago. He could also tell that the squirrel had been nervous, running this way and that.

The detective huffed and puffed his way through the snow. His breath came in clouds from his wide mouth.

The track led to a tall pine tree with a hole in it—a small hole to crawl in through and a large hole inside. The squirrel had gathered nuts all autumn and stored them there. He had been planning to eat them in winter. But many of the nuts had been stolen.

"Come and look!" the agitated squirrel called from up in the hole.

"No," said the detective. "I—I—hmm, I'm reluctant to climb trees."

"This many have been stolen!" cried the squirrel, making wild gestures with his arms.

"Oh," said the detective. "Oh dear."

In the snow on the ground below, the detective could see exactly what had happened when the squirrel discovered the theft. He had run back and forth. A little here, a little there, then here, and there again.

"Hmm," said the detective, bending down to inspect something.

"Is it tracks from the thief?" asked the squirrel.

"No, I think it is—hmm...did you cry when you discovered the theft?"

The squirrel nodded in silence.

"It's a frozen tear," said the detective. "Do you live in this hole?"

The squirrel shook his head. He lived in another tree. He had only been here to his pantry to count his nuts. Just to be on the safe side.

"And how often do you count your nuts?"

The squirrel apparently counted them every Sunday.

"Hmm," said the detective. "Then the theft could have taken place several days ago. The thief, therefore, has an advantage. And the ground is covered in fresh snow, so there are no tracks from the thief. By the way, do you have many of these hidden pantries?"

The squirrel nodded. Many.

"Best you go home now so you don't freeze. I'll keep watch. Rest assured, dear squirrel!"

The squirrel went off through the snow. Then he came back to return the handkerchief he had borrowed. The detective laid the small frozen tear in it.

The squirrel scurried off again.

The detective sat down in the snow and watched. He looked at the hole.

With his eyes fixed on it, he began to think.

Squirrels are a little scatter-brained, he thought. They forget things and you can't always rely on what they say. But this one is probably telling the truth.

Someone really had stolen a lot of his nuts. And this thief had also stolen others' nuts. Recent complaints had been received from a woodpecker, a field mouse, and a jay. The detective had written all the complaints down on paper and stamped them.

Their stories weren't all confused and vague and incomplete. A major thief was clearly at work, plundering in this forest. And it was up to Detective Gordon to catch it!

But all he could do for the moment was to keep his eyes strictly on the hole. It was a shame he was the only policeman at the station. The snow kept falling and he thought about tea and cakes.

He stared crossly at the hole.

Detective Gordon never looked crossly at anyone. But it didn't hurt to be cross with a hole. To pass the time, he thought more about cakes and very hot tea. The snow went on falling, covering the detective in white powder.

He tried to look sternly and commandingly at the hole. It didn't help. The hole was giving nothing away.

The detective thought about a warm fire and his paper with the important notes on it.

Afterwards he would write in his report:

Watched the hole. Nothing happened.

The detective hated sitting in the snow, watching.

Worst of all, his arms and legs were almost frozen solid.

Now he had completely disappeared under the snow.

And he fell asleep.

He woke with a little shudder. He'd heard a noise from the hole and his eyes flew open. He stared at the hole. Was his patient surveillance about to pay off? Was he about to catch the thief?

Something appeared in the hole. What was it? He blinked a few times.

A mouse. A little mouse. And the mouse had a nut in its arms.

Ha, he thought. Here we have a significant thief, and the significant thief is a little mouse!

"Stop! In the name of the law!" called the detective in an icy voice.

Yes, his voice was icy. The entire Detective Gordon was ice-cold.

The little mouse hopped lightly to the ground and began to scamper away as fast as it could.

"I'll catch you!" shouted the detective.

That was when he discovered that he had frozen solid.

Interrogation
of the suspect.

The mouse disappeared. Detective Gordon could just make out the top of the brown nut bouncing away through the snow. But the detective was stuck, with frozen fingers and toes.

"Help! In the name of the law!" cried the detective.

Then he added a little more gently:

"Please!"

The nut stopped bouncing. It was motionless. And then it came back, hesitantly.

The nut drew closer. Beneath it was a small and very young mouse.

"Good evening," said the detective.

"Good evening," said the mouse.

The detective cleared his throat.

"Could you help me up, please?"

The mouse put down the nut and began to brush snow from the detective. It tried to free one of his legs.

"Ouch," said the Detective Gordon.

The mouse began to dig with its tiny hands. Now and then it blew on its palms to warm them. The mouse managed to free one of the detective's legs. The leg was strong and covered in warts. The foot had webbing between the long toes, which were blue with cold.

The mouse shuddered a little and dug out an arm. Then Detective Gordon was able to help free the rest of himself.

"I won't write it in my report," he said, clearing his throat. "That I was frozen solid like that…"

"I'm terribly hungry," said the mouse. "Am I allowed to eat this nut?"

"Hmm, you might as well," said the detective.

Terribly hungry? he thought. That would mean the mouse wasn't a significant thief. A significant thief who had stolen hundreds of nuts wouldn't be walking around hungry. Besides, a little mouse was rarely a significant thief.

The mouse quickly gnawed a nice little hole in the top of the nutshell. It poked in its tiny arm and pulled out the nut. Then it ate the entire nut in a thousand small, quick bites, its eyes closed in pleasure.

"I must ask you to come with me to the police station," said the detective firmly.

The mouse said nothing.

The detective stood with difficulty. He was mighty cold and stiff and his legs seemed to creak and tremble when he straightened them.

"I must also ask you to help me get to the police station," the detective said.

The mouse supported him and they limped slowly onto the path and down to the police station where a light still shone in the window. The detective opened the door.

The mouse hesitated on the threshold. The little creature looked around anxiously.

"No one's here," said the detective. "I'm the only policeman in the forest. It's just me. Sadly."

The detective set to work, lighting the fire in the wood stove and putting on the kettle. Meanwhile, the mouse sat on the visitors' stool, dangling its legs.

When the detective had made tea, he took four cakes from one of the big tins.

"These are the evening and night cakes," he said.

They were chocolate cakes with blackcurrant jam. He served up two each, then he sat in his swivel chair opposite the mouse.

"I don't think you're a thief," said the detective.

"No, I was just hungry," answered the mouse. "I was so hungry, I was dizzy and faint. My stomach was so empty, it hurt. It seemed unfair that I had nothing to eat…"

The detective blinked his big eyes. He could imagine how awful that would be.

"And then I was terrified when you called out in that icy voice," the mouse continued.

"Terrible to be hungry," said the detective, shaking his head so that his chins quivered. "I shall take notes on our interview. How old are you?"

"No years old," said the mouse, and Detective Gordon wrote down zero.

"What is your name?"

"I don't have a name," said the mouse. "I'm just a baby mouse."

The detective wrote another zero.

"Where do you live?"

"Nowhere."

Another zero.

"And what is your occupation?"

The mouse shrugged its shoulders. "I don't have one."

The detective wrote yet another zero.

Then he looked hard at what he'd written.

0 0 0 0

The detective sighed.

"This is simply awful. Four zeros! But you must have a name, at least. Without a name you're a kind of nobody. Without a name you hardly exist."

The mouse looked at its hands and moved them back and forth. Do I not exist? it wondered. It looked anxiously at the detective who had begun to swivel in his stylish chair.

The detective had always taken pride in being a toad. And he was very proud of his fine name, Gordon. But there were two other names he considered especially beautiful. Buffy and Todd.

Now he would choose the perfect one. He thought hard and swung right around in his chair. It squeaked.

"I'm a girl, by the way," said the mouse.

Aha, that made it easier.

"Your name will be Buffy," said the detective. "It's a beautiful name!"

The mouse looked very happy with her new name. Or was she simply glad that she existed?

"Buffy," said the mouse. "That's me!"

The detective drank the last of his tea and felt comfortably warm again. He wrote BUFFY on his paper. Then he took out his big stamp. He placed it in the middle of the paper, hesitated, and moved the stamp a little. Then he moved it back again. And pressed. Kla-dunk.

Buffy laughed happily.

Employing a
police assistant.

Detective Gordon suddenly felt very tired. Buffy
yawned, too. The night was almost finished. Soon it
would be a new day.

"You must get some sleep," said the detective.
"If you have nowhere to go, there's a bed here."

He moved toward the room in the police station
with bars on the door and window.

"You can sleep in here," he said.

"It's a prison," Buffy said quietly.

"It's a nice soft bed and the room is quiet and…"
The detective stopped when he noticed that Buffy
was crying.

"What's the matter?" He put his arm around
the mouse.

"I don't want to go to prison," said Buffy, sniffing.

The detective took the mouse to the other little room in the police station. It was his own bedroom.

"You can sleep in my room, and I'll sleep in the prison."

"Can't we both sleep in the prison?"

"Of course," said the detective.

So they carried the detective's bed into the prison. And then they lay down side by side, each in their own bed.

The detective turned out the light.

"Good night," he said.

"Good night," said Buffy.

Detective Gordon lay thinking over the terrible night. First he had been forced to go on a mission in the dark forest when everyone else was asleep. Then he had failed to climb the tree to inspect the scene of the crime. Dreadful! And then he had frozen solid in the snow. A horrible night.

Detective Gordon didn't like horrible things. What he liked most was a warm fire, a cup of tea, and a few cakes, preferably with blackcurrant jam. Ideally he would like nothing to happen at all.

But he was a clever detective, of course. He was good at listening to squirrels and writing reports. And he was good at thinking. But perhaps someone could help him with the hard police work, such as climbing and keeping watch, he thought. Perhaps someone younger and slimmer.

A little while later, just before he fell asleep, the Detective Gordon suddenly had an idea.

"Would you like to be a policeman, by the way?"

"Be a what?"

"A policema—woman!"

"Yes!" said Buffy without a second thought.

"Then I will employ you as a policewoman."

"Yes, yes!" said Buffy in the dark.

"But there is one thing…" continued the detective, clearing his throat. "You mustn't forget that I am the chief of police. And that you are my assistant."

"Yes, chief!" answered Buffy.

It was quiet for a moment. In the dark, the detective heard Buffy giggling with happiness.

"Tomorrow we have a difficult task, maybe the hardest we've had so far. We must track down the real thief and catch him. Or her. Or them."

"We can do it, chief," said Buffy.

Then it was quiet for a long time.

"Is it really true that I'm a policewoman, chief?"

The detective climbed out of bed and disappeared into the dark office. He went to the desk, lit dimly by the moon.

Buffy heard the chair squeak. And then she heard the big stamp being placed on paper, moved a little, and then moved back again. Kla-dunk.

Buffy bubbled over inside.

"Good night, chief."

The detective came back and climbed into his bed.

"Good night."

Both of them fell straight asleep.

Investigating
new tracks.

Next morning Detective Gordon woke from a dream.
He had dreamed that he was running along a path. He
ran faster than a deer. And he climbed a tree as nimbly
as a squirrel.

"Wretched robbers," someone cried in a shaky
voice. "Robbing wretches! Hoo!"

The detective didn't open his eyes immediately. He
wanted to stay in his lovely dream. Who was that,
waking him?

"Villainous thieves!" cried the little creature.
"Thieving villains!"

It must be the squirrel, thought the detective.

He opened his big round eyes.

It was the squirrel.

"Good morning," said the detective.

"The thieves have been there again!" said the agitated squirrel.

Detective Gordon thought about his night vigil and how he caught Buffy, the little mouse.

"No, really," he said, "it was only a single little nut for a hungry indiv—"

"They've taken each and every single one. The whole lot," cried the squirrel. "Good morning, by the way."

Then the squirrel caught sight of Buffy lying in the other bed. Only her nose and whiskers showed above the eiderdown. Buffy was asleep.

The squirrel stared.

"Is that the thief? And you caught it? And put it in prison? And now you're guarding it?"

The detective explained that he had hired an assistant to help him solve the case quickly. And that the two of them would come as soon as they had eaten breakfast.

The squirrel showed no sign of leaving. He had clearly decided to stay. But the detective didn't want to get out of bed until he was alone.

"Off you go," he said briskly. "Hurry now and guard the tracks. Don't touch anything!"

The squirrel hurried off. And the detective got up slowly, with difficulty. He stood bent over by the bed, breathing heavily. He had been so light and quick in his dream…

Then he got dressed and put the kettle on.

"Up you get, Buffy. We have a thief to track down…"

Before he had finished his sentence, Buffy jumped out of bed and saluted. She was already dressed.

"Good morning, chief!" she said in a cheerful voice.

"Good morning. Now we're going to have a little morning cake. They're kept in the second big tin, the morning tin."

He opened the lid and set out four cakes. Vanilla cakes with strawberry jam.

"What's in the third big tin, chief?"

"You'll find out soon enough."

They ate in peace and quiet, especially enjoying the jam.

As they got ready to leave, Buffy asked, "Shall we take the pistol, chief?"

"No," the detective said quickly, "not the pistol!"

They trudged through the snow. The sun shone, but it was cold and the detective regretted leaving his gloves behind.

All the animals were awake now. A magpie and a crow were bickering. Sparrows were foraging in the treetops, and there were rabbits digging in the snow. The detective and his assistant saluted them all.

They came to the hole in the pine tree and the detective gave it a bitter look. The squirrel already sat in the hole, complaining. Buffy scampered up.

What a sprightly and clever little assistant I have, the detective thought proudly.

"Bravo!" he said when the mouse reached the hole.

The two above him looked down in surprise. "Bravo what?" they wondered.

"The hole's very empty, chief."

"Hmm," said the detective. "Are the nuts gone?"

"The nuts are very gone, chief!"

Buffy climbed down and the two police officers began to investigate the tracks in the snow. This alleged burglary had occurred in fresh snow. That was perfectly clear. A number of tracks led to the path, where they disappeared into an even greater number of tracks.

Somebody had gone back and forth between the hole and the path with stolen nuts. Who? Or what?

Detective Gordon kneeled low to look at the tracks more closely.

"Bother and dash!" he burst out.

"What's dash, chief?"

"You don't need to call me 'chief' every time," the detective whispered.

"Thank you. It's quite hard to say 'dash, chief.'"

"The problem is that the thieves have deliberately concealed their tracks. First they ran back and forth with the nuts. Then they dragged a fir branch over the tracks, to wipe out the footprints…"

The squirrel stood beside him, wringing his hands.

"Will I get my nuts back?"

The detective gave him a sharp look and raised his index finger slightly.

"We must think," he continued.

He walked around, hmming grumpily. He bent down again. He went over the trail and hmmed more crossly. Then he found a fir branch beside the trail, checked it carefully, and his hmm sounded almost pleased. He then went for a long walk in the forest, looking hard at trees until at last he said, "Ha!"

He came back smiling.

"Now I think we can draw some conclusions."

The squirrel was about to ask something, but the detective raised his finger.

CHAPTER · SIX

The assistant goes tracking on her own.

"This is how it works!" said Detective Gordon.

He explained that two quite small animals had carried out the theft together. They had planned it. They were aware that it was a crime to steal. They didn't want to be discovered and they were very smart.

The squirrel and the mouse were dumbfounded.

"How, how, how?" stammered Buffy.

The detective explained his thinking. Anyone who dragged a fir branch over his tracks did it to conceal them. Therefore he or she knew it was wrong to steal.

When the detective had looked carefully at the snowy white fir branch, he had noticed that the snow had melted in two places on each end, where small hands had grabbed the branch to drag it over the tracks. Therefore there were two of them.

Furthermore, the fir branch had been taken from a small tree quite a way off in the forest, and they had brought it with them. Therefore it was planned. And therefore they were smart.

"Bravo!" Buffy felt proud of her chief.

"We can rule out that this is a poor, small, hungry thief who has taken one nut. These are significant thieves."

"Significant thieves should be in prison!" The squirrel was upset. "And small thieves too, by the way!"

Buffy blushed.

The detective said, "I think that whoever stole because she was so hungry that her stomach ached has not committed a very serious crime."

"Why not?" protested the squirrel. "One way or the other, the nuts are gone. Think of the poor owner who's missing his little nut. I won't get it back just because it was a small thief who ate it."

Detective Gordon raised his finger and the squirrel was quiet. Sometimes he couldn't help interrupting.

"How many nuts do you own?"

"Fifteen thousand, seven hundred and four," the squirrel said quickly. "One-five-seven-oh-four."

The detective nodded.

"We must have a forest where everybody is happy," he said. "The crime shall be punished. But if someone is in trouble—say they're dizzy and about to faint and need a bite to eat—we're understanding. We must make allowances in our forest. All of us."

"All of us! Allowances!" the squirrel scoffed. "Now I'm so angry I can't speak. I'm going."

And off he went, striding for home. Buffy breathed out.

"It can't be just any animal who's done this," the detective said to Buffy. "Hmm."

Buffy scratched behind her ear and thought: who could it be?

She thought about rabbits, beavers, birds. No, not birds; they would have flown.

She thought about hares, hedgehogs, bumblebees. No, not bumblebees. There were hardly any bumblebees around in winter.

Then she found herself thinking about the most dangerous animal of all. The most dangerous and the most cunning. Then she thought about two such animals. Two dangerous and cunning animals!

Buffy grew very scared. She needed to make a dangerous and important investigation. The very thought made her shiver. But she must do it regardless. Buffy was a policewoman now. She had to show that she was up to it. And she had to pay for that old nut somehow.

"Chief, I have an idea," she said. "I think we need to cover a lot more ground in our search, through deep snow, down into narrow dens, and up into tall trees."

Detective Gordon sighed deeply. He was already very tired.

"Chief, I think I need to do this alone."

The detective breathed out and smiled.

"Bravo!" he said. "How courageous you are. While you're at it, I'll go home and make a list of suspects. And do some stamping. I'll warm some milk for when you come home. And we'll eat lunch cakes from the last big tin."

Buffy wanted to ask something, but Detective Gordon merely raised his finger.

So the two police officers went their separate ways.

Buffy had a plan. She wanted to interrogate a lot of mice, rabbits, and hares. She would ask them if they thought the most dangerous and cunning animal had stolen the nuts.

She visited all the animals she knew. She wormed along tunnels to the nests of field mice, who nodded gravely when she asked them. She burrowed down into sandy rabbit holes and the rabbits also nodded gravely. She scampered over vast fields chasing hares, who also agreed that it would be typical of the most dangerous and cunning animal to steal nuts now as well.

Buffy felt sure.

Now it was time for the second part of her plan.

She climbed high into a tree and spoke with
sparrows, wrens, and finches. She gathered ten small
birds around her. In a whisper she instructed them to
fly out in every direction and look for the most
dangerous and cunning creature. Even a long way away.

"Go and look! In the name of the law!"

She felt very proud saying this. All the birds fluttered
up and disappeared on command, off to survey the
whole forest and then report back to Buffy with the
whereabouts of the most dangerous and cunning animal.

And soon she received her answer.

A little wren came flying, out of breath. The most
dangerous and cunning creature had been found in his
hideout. It was a very long way away.

Now for the third part of her plan.

Buffy had no time to lose. With a pounding heart, she set off. The hideout was beyond the forest, beyond Detective Gordon's precinct. But the law knew no bounds. The police must catch thieves wherever they might hide.

After a long time, Buffy arrived. She slipped down into the lair itself. Her heart was still pounding, from fear and excitement. She was so scared that her tail trembled, but she crept on through the dugout. The smell was dreadful.

Deeper and deeper she went. It grew darker and darker.

At last she spied the most dangerous and cunning animal, fast asleep. She smelled its bitter stench. She saw its sharp teeth.

Buffy tiptoed bravely around, looking through the entire lair. But she couldn't find any nuts.

The thief had probably hidden them somewhere else. He was very cunning!

Then she sneaked quietly out again. Outside in the snow, she breathed the fresh, cold air to calm herself. She was very pleased with what she'd done, and she rushed home to the detective.

Her heart was pounding with anticipation.

The police think and stamp.

When Buffy returned, she reported to Detective Gordon.

She sat on the visitors' stool and the detective was in his swivel chair. He didn't interrupt her once. He just nodded and made notes on his paper.

"The fox?" The detective said at last.

"Yes," said Buffy. "The most dangerous and cunning animal. Let's go and get him now. And put him in prison."

"How do we get him?" asked the detective.

"We take the pistol and the baton. I can manage the pistol," said Buffy. "But not the baton."

"No," said the detective. "Not the pistol."

He swivelled in his chair. It squeaked.

"May I sit for a moment in the swivel chair?" asked Buffy.

"No," said the detective. "This is the chief's chair. But we can move the visitors' stool over so we're both sitting on the same side."

They carried the stool over. They both sat with their elbows on the table, heads in hands. They kept thinking until the detective stood up.

"It's time for warm milk and lunch cakes."

He took four cakes from the final tin. Oat cakes with bits of candied orange.

The lunchtime cakes were very good, they agreed.

The detective said, "Buffy, you're young, quick, and good at running, climbing, and tracking. I'm very proud of you."

"Thank you," said Buffy.

"But," the detective continued, "you must understand that I'm old. Nineteen years old."

"Whew."

The detective pretended not to hear. He patted his belly and grabbed a thick roll in both hands.

"I'm perhaps not so limber," he said, "but I have experience. I once had to deal with the fox. He was being very unpleasant to the mice and rabbits in our forest. I was the one who got him to move to another forest."

"How?" said Buffy with admiration.

"It is perhaps my most important case. The most beautiful. I'll tell you about it another time. But right now I can tell you that however horrible the fox may be, he definitely hasn't climbed trees or stolen nuts."

Buffy was silent.

The detective showed her the list he had made. The animals who could be suspects were in one column. Beside it, crosses were placed here and there in more columns.

If a particular animal had a cross in the first column, it meant "this animal likes nuts."

A cross in the second column meant "can climb trees."

The third column meant "makes tracks in snow."

The detective pointed to FOX. It had just one cross: "makes tracks in snow."

"The fox doesn't eat nuts and can't climb. The fox is eliminated. Experience, you see!" The detective kneaded his belly roll.

"Hedgehog," said Buffy. "What if it's a hedgehog?"

The detective shook his head and pointed to the list. It read "sleeps during winter."

"But who has three crosses?" asked Buffy.

The detective looked carefully.

"Mice," he said, ominously. "And squirrels."

"Squirrels? But that's who…"

"There are many squirrels in the forest. Right now, all are suspects," said the detective, taking out the stamp.

He placed it in the middle of the paper. He checked carefully, moved it a little, and then moved it back. And pressed. Kla-dunk!

Buffy stood up eagerly.

"May I stamp?"

"No, not yet! Stamping is not allowed until you've received full police training. Or until you work out how to solve this case," said the detective, peering down his nose at her.

"Can't you give me full police training?" Buffy asked. "Teach me how to catch wretched thieves and…"

"Just hear what I say," said the detective. "And do as I do!"

They sat and thought, each resting their head on one hand. When the detective changed hands, so did Buffy. When the detective sighed, Buffy sighed, too. The detective fetched two extra lunch cakes and placed them in the middle of the desk.

"We can have them when we come up with something."

Both frowned deeply. The detective appeared to close his eyes. And Buffy scratched behind her ear.

She badly wanted a cake. Her slim little arm crept across the table. The detective's eyes were closed. She was about to snatch one when the detective lifted his finger and said, "I see you!"

Just then Buffy had an idea and she brightened.

She pulled the detective close and whispered in his ear.

"Yes," said Detective Gordon. "You've come up with a fresh new idea! That's what we'll do! And now you may stamp!"

Buffy took the stamp from the drawer, and placed it carefully on the paper. And even more carefully than the detective, she moved it a smidgeon to the right and then a smidgeon to the left. And she pressed. Kla-dunk! She smiled proudly.

"Bravo," said the detective. "I am very proud of you."

And then the two police friends ate the two cakes.

CHAPTER EIGHT

One trap.
One thief.

Detective Gordon thought Buffy's idea was excellent.
It had something to do with the cakes on the table.
And with someone who closed their eyes and
someone who was peckish.

In other words, it was a trap!

First they had to borrow twenty nuts from various
mice and squirrels.

Then they would make a beautiful nut pyramid
beside the path in the forest.

They would write on a sign: These nuts belong to
Buffy. Taking these nuts is absolutely forbidden.

The significant thief might fall into the trap. He might sneak up and take off with the nuts. Or she might. Or they.

But then Detective Gordon and Buffy would sneak after them and see where the nuts were hidden.

They would catch the thief. Or thieves. And they would get the squirrel's nuts back.

Buffy was so pleased with her idea that she giggled constantly as they planned.

They had to make one or two small changes.

"We can't borrow the nuts," said the detective. "In case the mice and squirrels become suspicious. We'd be borrowing them from the very types who could be our thieves. And they might not fall for our trap…"

"We can borrow them from another forest, in another police district!" said Buffy.

"We could make the nut pyramid right outside the police station's window," said the detective. "Then I can quietly drink tea and look out through the window."

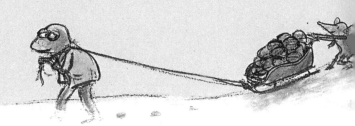

"No, for cats' sake!" said Buffy. "No thief would dare to steal right outside a police station."

The detective was a little hurt. After all, he was the chief of police. And "cats' sake" is the worst thing a mouse can say.

Buffy noticed the detective's face clouding over.

"But that's a very good idea," she said. "We can place the pyramid a tiny bit further away, but so you can still see it from the window. And then I'll make tea for you."

The detective was a little happier.

They took a toboggan and went to another forest. Not the one where the fox lived, but in the other direction. There they found a family of field mice who could lend them twenty top-quality hazelnuts. They pulled their heavy load back home again.

The detective wrote the sign. He thought for a moment of putting the stamp on it, but that might be going a bit far. Still, it was a very fine stamp, with the words Detective Gordon in it. In the middle was a royal crown. The detective didn't actually know what the crown was doing there, but it seemed powerful and no one had questioned it.

Buffy stacked the nuts into a beautiful pyramid a little way from the police station. The detective pushed the sign into the snow.

The sun went down. It began to get dark. It was the perfect time for thieves! Dark enough for them to dare to steal, but light enough for them to read the sign and understand that these nuts belonged to someone else.

The detective sat at the window. He was tired. It had been unusually hard work pulling the nuts on the toboggan, perhaps because he hadn't done it before.

While the water was still simmering in the kettle, he fell asleep. His head drooped and hit the windowsill. But with Buffy there, he couldn't admit it had happened, so he cleared his throat slightly and swept up a little earth that had fallen from the pot of geraniums.

There was going to be a bump on his forehead.

As they drank tea at the window, he perked up. They ate their evening and night cakes, the dark ones with blackcurrant jam.

"It's good to have different cakes at different times," said the detective. "Police work goes on all hours of day and night, but according to the type of cake you know what time it is."

Buffy stowed that away in her memory because she enjoyed police work and wanted to be a detective one day. Maybe even chief of police...

Then Detective Gordon fell asleep again. But this time he had leaned back because he didn't want to hit his bumped head again. He woke to hear himself snoring. Embarrassing! Buffy didn't seem to have noticed, but she was smiling to herself.

"I have a slightly sore throat," said the detective, in case she had heard any strange sounds.

He was about to fall asleep again, this time to one side, but he didn't get there because Buffy cried, "There's the thief!"

And so it was. Out in the night, a dark figure was picking nuts from the pile.

Quick as a wink, the detective was on his feet. He even managed to answer Buffy before she'd asked the question: "No, not the pistol."

A thief goes to prison.
For a moment.

They went out into the snow. It was very cold outside. The chill bit their cheeks and they looked like two puffing steam engines.

Then they had to creep after the thief. Quietly, quietly was the way to do it. They saw him up ahead with four nuts in his arms. He was following the path. Or she.

Then he trudged into the forest. And over to the pine tree with the hole in it.

"What?"

Now the thief began to climb. It was clearly very difficult with four nuts. Wasn't it a squirrel?

"Stop! In the name of the law!" called Detective Gordon and Buffy at the same time.

It was a squirrel! It was the squirrel himself. And he was so scared that nuts flew everywhere.

"Help!" cried the squirrel.

The detective went over to him and said, "Squirrel. You're under arrest for theft! Come with me at once to the prison."

The squirrel started to cry. Tears rolled down his soft cheeks where they immediately froze to ice. Small pearls fell to the ground.

"Bother," said the detective. "Come with me now, and you can have a cup of tea. But you'll have to carry the nuts back all by yourself."

When they got back, Buffy stacked them in the pyramid.

By the time they reached the police station, the squirrel had regained his courage. He was even plucky.

"You don't really think I've stolen my own nuts?" he said.

"We think only that you've stolen nuts from our pile," said the detective. "Now we need to question you. I'm sorry but you'll have to sit on the floor."

The squirrel sat down and stared crossly at the police.

"What is your name?" asked Buffy.

"Vladimir," said the squirrel.

The detective took notes.

"Where do you live?"

"Dash it, you know where I live! Just over there."

The detective wrote that down.

"Why did you steal our nuts?" asked Buffy.

The squirrel sighed. Then he started a long story.

"You don't understand how much I miss my lost nuts. I have 15,704 nuts. But 204 of them have been gone since last night. It's like having 204 small children who failed to come home. And I don't know where they're living. Are they all right or are they suffering? I miss them so much, and I can't think about anything but my lost nuts. Don't you have children of your own?"

Both shook their heads.

The squirrel continued his complicated story. Sometimes the detective didn't know if he was talking about real children or about nuts. Sometimes new creatures appeared in the hole in the tree, or perhaps they were nuts, and then they disappeared again.

The detective didn't interrupt. Neither did Buffy. She wanted to become a proper policewoman.

Sometimes they said a small "Uh-huh" to keep the squirrel going.

The squirrel knew all his nuts by sight, he said. He had names for them all. He even celebrated their birthdays.

"Don't you eat them?" asked Buffy.

"Yes," said the squirrel. "If I must. But only because of hunger."

Then the story continued. Now it was about love and passion.

"You know, of course, what love is?" asked the squirrel.

"I'm too old," said the detective with a sigh.

"I'm too young," said Buffy.

"Oh, it pains my heart so much to lose the only thing that matters to a squirrel. Nuts."

And he went on like this until the detective fell asleep onto the desk and cried "Ouch" because he had landed right on his bump.

"I've hardly slept the last few nights," he explained, feeling ashamed.

Now the police had to decide. What should they do?

"You who love nuts so much," said the detective, "you of all people should understand what it feels like to have them stolen. Especially when there's a sign. Now you must sit in prison…"

The squirrel's face grew longer and he was on the verge of tears again.

"…for a moment!" said the detective. "A quarter of an hour or so. You can take whichever bed you choose. And you'll think about how someone feels when they've been burgled."

"I can lock the door," said Buffy.

"No," said the detective. "I don't like locked prisons."

"Can I do the stamping then?"

"No," said the detective shortly. "It's my turn."

The detective was always a little grumpy when he was tired. He stamped very carefully, moving the stamp a little here, a little there. Kla-dunk!

The squirrel called Vladimir walked dejectedly into the prison. His tail dragged on the floor.

Then Buffy noticed something outside the window. She whispered excitedly to the detective, "There are the thieves!"

The real
thieves.

Detective Gordon and Buffy came out into the snow.
It took a moment for their eyes to adjust to the dark.
But then they made out two dark figures, laughing.
One of them pulled up the sign, read it, burst out in a
braying laugh, and threw it on the ground.

"It's the real thieves," said Buffy.

"I'm sorry to say it is," said the detective.

The thieves loaded themselves up with nuts and
went staggering off. The two police followed.

Phew, how cold it was now! The detective regretted
leaving his gloves behind.

They had gone a fair way when Buffy stopped.

"We really must take the pistol with us, chief!"

"No, not the pistol!"

"Why not? Why do you always say that?"

The detective put his hands on his hips and looked gravely at Buffy.

"To take the pistol one must be very wise and very careful. It's dangerous."

Buffy jumped up and down angrily. The thieves were disappearing between the trees. But she badly wanted them to have the pistol.

She would have it.

"But you're very wise and very careful, chief."

Detective Gordon held up his finger. He had something important to say.

"The one who is really wise and very careful doesn't take it with him!" said the detective. "It's dangerous."

Far, far away they could hear the thieves laughing. But Buffy wouldn't give up.

"Why is it in the glass cabinet then? Why don't you throw it away?"

"In case someone finds it and hurts themselves. It is safest locked up in the police station."

Now they finally went on. They followed the tracks. Buffy ran ahead.

The detective found it very difficult to hurry in snow.

His big flat feet got in the way. What's more, they were slippery.

A toad should sleep in peace and quiet through the winter, he thought. It's against nature to carry on like this.

Just then he slipped on a patch of ice and fell on his bottom. Ouch.

He happened to be on a hillside and he began to slide. Oops.

Faster and faster he went. Uh-oh!

He slid full speed into a scrubby bush. Ouff!

Buffy ran over to him.

"Hurry and see where the thieves live!" said the detective, trying to sound heroic. "Just leave me here…"

"No way. Not on your life."

"But I'm stuck in a bush and I have sore feet and I'm tired. I'm no use to you."

"We police always stick together," said Buffy. "I'll pull you out. And then I'll carry you…"

She thought about that and changed her mind.

"Support you, I mean. You can't let me do this on my own. Some of us are faster than others. But you're indispensable! We police need someone who's big, wise, and has a very powerful voice."

The detective felt his heart grow warm and he began working his way out. Buffy pulled his arm.

It was a relentless struggle against small scrubby branches that jabbed and clung. But at last the detective was free of the bush. They limped along, following the tracks of the thieves.

They arrived at a large oak tree with a big hole in it. The thieves were inside—the police could tell because of the cheerful laughter. It was surely the hideout.

"Come out! In the name of the law!" called the detective and his voice was so powerful that he almost frightened himself.

Two grinning faces appeared in the hole. They were indeed two squirrels.

"You're the ones who have stolen Buffy's twenty nuts!" called the detective.

"Ha-ha-ha!" came from inside the hole.

"And stolen Vladimir's 204 nuts."

"Ha-ha-ha!"

"And the nuts of woodpeckers and jays and mice."

"Ha-ha-ha!"

The detective and Buffy looked at one another. They nodded. The two squirrels had practically admitted to the crime.

The detective knew what the squirrels were thinking. They were thinking "Ha-ha-ha, we're so clever!" And they were probably thinking, "Finders, keepers" and "If you can sit on it, you own it!" and "Ha-ha-ha, we're so smart!"

The detective could practically hear the thoughts behind their boisterous laughter: "We can take whatever we want." But that would never be so in his police district.

"Come down! In the name of the law!" called the detective. "We must ask you to come with us to the prison."

Up in the hole, the two squirrels began to laugh even harder.

And they started to nail and hammer sticks across the hole so no one could come in. When they'd finished, they looked like bars. Prison bars.

"Ha-ha-ha!" they called. "You can't get us and we're not coming out!"

Buffy and the detective looked at one another in surprise.

"They've put themselves in prison," said Buffy.

"That works quite well," said the detective after a moment. "In fact, it's much better! Though it's always a little sad when people put themselves in prison…"

Then Buffy suddenly did something curious. She started to dance around and around in front of the hole.

She hummed an annoying rhyme: "Nah-na-na-na-nah-na. You can't hit me-ee!"

For a moment nothing happened in the hole. Then a nut came flying through the bars.

"You missed me, you missed me!" sang Buffy.

A swarm of nuts came flying!

CHAPTER ELEVEN

224 nuts.

It was chaos. Many of the forest animals had been woken up and came to watch. Nuts were flying from the hole. And the hole looked exactly like a prison.

The animals stood in a ring around the oak tree and the white snow was peppered with hazelnuts.

"Stop!" called Detective Gordon. "You've thrown out exactly 224 nuts. The exact number you've stolen."

The two squirrels grumbled between themselves. They knew they'd been tricked.

"How many nuts do you have left?" asked the detective.

"12,417," shouted the squirrels, and they laughed.

"Then there's nothing more to be done with you," said the detective. "You can stay inside and eat nuts. And you can think about how it feels to be burgled."

The squirrels weren't sure whether to laugh or

complain. Imagine sitting in your nest eating nuts—
what could be better? They didn't actually need to go
out. But were they truly not allowed to go out? And
did they really have to think the whole time about
people who'd lost their nuts?

They couldn't decide what to think, so they laughed
impudently at the detective.

"Ha-ha-ha!"

"So, we can go back now and stamp our papers,"
said Buffy, nodding.

All the animals helped to gather up the nuts and
carry them to the police station. They made one pile
of twenty nuts for the detective and Buffy to return by
toboggan to the field mice. And another big pile of
204 nuts belonging to Vladimir.

"Thank you very much, all you animals," said the
two police friends and they saluted.

It was lovely to come back to
the police station. The
detective put more wood
on the fire and the
embers caught flame.
Lovely and warm. Then
he put on the kettle.

"Which cakes now?" asked the detective.

"Evening and night cakes," said Buffy.

They heard someone snoring. The squirrel Vladimir was still asleep in the prison.

"Tell him it's time for tea and cakes," said the detective.

After a while the dozy squirrel came out.

"Can I have my nuts? What happened to my nuts?" he asked, confused.

Buffy pointed out the window.

"I can't believe it. How happy I am," said the squirrel, almost in tears. "At last, my sorrow is over!"

The detective shook his head and poured tea into three cups.

Then the squirrel's face changed. Suddenly he looked grim.

"Those wretched thieves," he said. "Where are those thieving wretches?"

"The thieves have been caught, have admitted their crime, and paid their debt," said the detective. "They're sitting, to some degree, in prison. But one can say that they are, yes, that they're completely…away."

"Completely away?"

"Drink some tea," said the detective.

"And eat a little cake!"

The squirrel ate a whole cake and asked for another. The cakes tasted so good and he loved blackcurrant jam, he said. It was almost as good as nuts. When he had finished eating he looked a little happier.

"I don't entirely understand," he said, blowing on his tea.

"One doesn't need to understand," said the detective, "as long as one feels that everything is all right."

The squirrel drank his tea.

"But I still want to see the thieves," he said. "I want to see what a thief looks like!"

The detective went and fetched the little mirror from the wall. The squirrel took it in confusion. He had never seen a mirror before. He didn't like modern gadgets.

He looked at the face in the mirror. He had never seen himself properly before. He glared at the image.

"He looks angry and a bit stingy and greedy!" said the squirrel.

"Yes," said the detective, "he can look a bit like that. But I think he can also look happy and kind."

The squirrel brightened a little.

"Perhaps," he said, when he looked at the image. "Perhaps somewhat kind."

The squirrel handed back the mirror.

"I don't understand modern contraptions. They make me dizzy," said the squirrel, going on his way. "Good night!"

"Good night, good night!"

The detective and Buffy remained behind the desk, drinking their tea.

They could hear the squirrel's voice out in the snow: "104, 105, 106, 107, 108, 109..."

Three
wishes.

Detective Gordon and Buffy felt very pleased with
themselves as they sat side by side behind the desk.
They were very happy. But they tried to look serious
and important, like proper police officers.

Suddenly the squirrel turned up again. He'd brought
a very big nut that he wanted to give them as a
present.

The detective and Buffy nodded at him somewhat
solemnly. Sitting there, they wanted to look serious and
important.

"This is a particularly fine and unusual nut I'm giving you as a present," said the squirrel. "A special gift. Almost certainly a double nut, and I'm missing it already, but I wanted to thank you very much."

He laid the hazelnut on the desk and bowed. The detective and Buffy bowed also. When the squirrel had closed the door behind him, Buffy took the nut and gnawed a large, beautifully even hole in its top. She stuck in her slender arm. And pulled out two nuts.

"A double nut," she said happily. "That means you can wish for two things."

Buffy said she thought it best that the detective made the wishes. She wanted them to be for important

things to do with police work, not just silly little things. Therefore someone with long experience should do the wishing.

Detective Gordon smiled solemnly, pressed his hands together, and cleared his throat.

"We two police wish for an end to crime. A good police district has no crime!"

"But don't we want lots of terrible thieves to catch?" asked Buffy. "Many difficult and exciting cases to solve?"

"No. The best thing would be if nothing happened, nothing at all!"

Buffy thought for a bit and nodded.

The detective thought about the fire, his tea cup, and the cake tins, and he sighed.

"We two police also wish not to apply punishments. The best case is when thieves punish themselves a little bit. And it's best for a prison to be comfortable. Where someone without a home can live. A police assistant, perhaps…"

Buffy agreed with all of this and the more she thought about it, the happier she felt.

The detective started to think about bed and was ready to nod off and fall asleep.

"You can wish for one more very small thing," said Buffy.

"In that case, I wish only that we can sleep in tomorrow for a long time."

The detective took out a piece of paper and wrote down the two real wishes:

"Let's both stamp it!" cried Buffy.

Together they took out the stamp and placed it on the paper. Buffy moved it a little to the right. The detective moved it a little to the left. Then they both pressed as hard as they could. KLA-DUNK!

"I shall keep this paper in the drawer for important notes," said the detective.

The two police friends shared a smile.

Together they had solved their first case.

They borrowed the nuts over there

The field where the hares live

The real thieves' big oak

224 nuts

Squirrel's hole no. 2

The rabbits' hole

Icy slope

Scrubby bush

Very small mouse holes here somewhere...

Squirrel's hole no. 1

Map of Detective Gordon's police district

Over there lives the dangerous and cunning fox

Squirrel's holes nos. 3 and 4

SCENE OF CRIME

Squirrel's hole no. 5

Footprints

Police station

BUFFY'S

Squirrel's hole no. 6

This edition first published in 2015 by Gecko Press
PO Box 9335, Marion Square, Wellington 6141, New Zealand
info@geckopress.com

First American edition published in 2015 by Gecko Press USA,
an imprint of Gecko Press Ltd. A catalog record for this book is available
from the US Library of Congress.

Distributed in the United States and Canada by Lerner Publishing Group,
www.lernerbooks.com
Distributed in the United Kingdom by Bounce Sales and Marketing,
www.bouncemarketing.co.uk
Distributed in Australia by Scholastic Australia,
www.scholastic.com.au
Distributed in New Zealand by Random House NZ,
www.randomhouse.co.nz

A catalogue record for this book is available from the National Library of New Zealand.

Original title: *Kommissarie Gordon: Det första fallet*
Text © Ulf Nilsson 2012
Illustrations © Gitte Spee 2012
First published by Bonnier Carlsen, Stockholm, Sweden
Published in the English language by arrangement with Bonnier Group Agency,
Stockholm, Sweden

The cost of this translation was defrayed by a subsidy from the Swedish Arts Council,
gratefully acknowledged.

Translated by Julia Marshall
Edited by Penelope Todd
Typesetting by Vida & Luke Kelly, New Zealand
Printed in China by Everbest Printing Co Ltd,
an accredited ISO 14001 & FSC certified printer

Hardback (USA) ISBN: 978-1-927271-49-0
Paperback ISBN: 978-1-927271-50-6
E-book available

For more curiously good books, visit www.geckopress.com